FRIENDS
POP QUIZ

Tim Tyrrell

Cover designed by Cover Designer

Tim Tyrrell
Visit my website at www.timtyrrell.com

Printed in the United States of America

First Printing: October 2022
Pop Quiz Books

ISBN-9798359250795

Other books by Tim Tyrrell

The Name Dropper

The Oliver Factor

8os Pop Quiz

1
Which character spoke the first line on the first episode?

2
What was the name of the place where Ross and Rachel got married in Las Vegas?

3
What was the name of the Gellar's dog that was sent to "live on the farm"?

4
Who played Missy Goldberg that Chandler and Ross went to college with?

5
What was the name of the monkey that Ross had?

6
What did everyone eat at their first Thanksgiving together in Monica's apartment?

7

What was the name of the 50-year-old librarian that Ross kissed in high school?

8

Who wound up being the owner of the furry handcuffs that Chandler found in the spare bedroom?

9

What was Ross's first choice for a boy's baby name with the child he was having with Rachel?

10

Who did Joey play on "Days of Our Lives"?

11

Which Friend gives the worst massages?

12

What did Rachel and Monica give their building super instead of tipping him for Christmas?

13
What does Phoebe find in a can of soda?

14
Who kissed Rachel's mother at Rachel's birthday party?

15
What did Joey keep saying that annoyed Chandler when they traveled for Ross
and Emily's wedding?

16
What actor delivered the line "well smack my ass and call me Judy"?

17
Who was considering purchasing the house next door to the one Monica and
Chandler were buying?

18
Where did Rachel buy the apothecary table that she put in Phoebe's apartment?

19

What did Ross wear on his date with Elizabeth Hornswaggle that he took off and could not get back on?

20

Who told Rachel about Ross sleeping with Chloe?

21

What actress played the pregnant woman that Joey helped the day Carol gave birth to Ben?

22

What kept Phoebe up all night in her apartment?

23

Who does everyone joke that Monica looks like in Barbados?

24

What does Rachel wear to attract Joshua that she says never misses?

25

What mistake did the bakery make for Emma's first birthday cake?

26

Who was the host of the game show that Joey was a guest on?

27

What name did Chandler give the chick?

28

What song did Phoebe's father make up when she was a child that was the same melody at "Smelly Cat"?

29

How many times did Rachel get off the plane to Paris?

30

What was the name of the guy Joey hired to be his identical twin for a medical research project?

31

What happened to Ross when Joey and Chandler took him to a hockey game?

32

What kind of car did Joey drive to Las Vegas when he got the lead in a movie?

33
What actress played Phoebe's birth mother that she found in Montauk?

34
What did Joey find in Rachel's bed when he took a nap?

35
Who went to Vermont with Chandler after Monica couldn't get off work?

36
What did Rachel get tattooed on her hip?

37
What was the name of Joey's stuffed penguin?

38
What did Mona bring Ross back from Atlantic City on the day she broke up with him?

39
What was the name of Phoebe's roommate that was never seen?

40

What book did Chandler buy Kathy for her birthday that he let Joey give to her?

41

What toy did Ben choose that freaked Ross out?

42

Who became Chandler's trainer after Phoebe told him he gained weight?

43

Who played Parker, the overly excited guy that Phoebe brought to Monica and Ross's parents 35th Anniversary party?

44

What did Joey call the acting technique where he takes a pause to think?

45

Who accidentally told Rachel that Ross was in love with her on her birthday?

46

What was Ross's reoccurring nightmare as a child that he saw a therapist for?

40

"The Velveteen Rabbit"

41

A doll

42

Monica

43

Alec Baldwin

44

Smell the fart acting

45

Chandler

46

That Monica was going to eat him

47
What was Monica's nickname when she was a field hockey goalie?

48
What event did Joey miss appearing in, even though he wrote himself a note on his arm?

49
Where did Rachel and Barry have sex at his workplace?

50
Which "Barney Miller" actor played Ross's divorce attorney?

51
Who made a pass at Phoebe while she was giving him a massage?

52
Who became an ordained minister on the internet?

53
What happened to Ross's wedding ring after he gave it to Joey?

54
What is the number of Monica's apartment?

55
Who was the first guy Rachel dated after finding out she was pregnant?

56
What is Joey's mother's first name?

57
What family heirloom did Phoebe's birth mother send her?

58
What song did Chandler and Phoebe sing after his break up with Janice?

59
What nickname did Ross have in high school that he blamed on a water fountain?

60
What secret did Joey tell Monica and Phoebe about the night he spent with his
date Ginger?

61

What is Ross's job title?

62

Where did the cheesecakes that Rachel and Chandler kept eating come from?

63

Who played Zack, Chandler's coworker that he hopes might be a sperm donor?

64

When Phoebe bought maternity clothes from a used clothing store, what kind of
pants did she buy?

65

Who did Ross hold up a banner for at Holidays on Ice at Madison Square Garden?

66

What was written on the back of the black leather jacket that Phoebe picked out
for Ross at Barney's?

67

What part of Chandler's body does his boss keep slapping?

68

What word does Ross keep saying when trying to move his couch up the stairs to his apartment?

69

What did Phoebe change her name to when she originally was going to add Mike's last name?

70

Who played Rachel's sister Jill?

71

Who got bit by a peacock at the zoo?

72

When Gary asked Phoebe to move in together, what part of the city did he want to move to?

73

When is Rachel's birthday?

74

How many States did Joey get in Chandler's name the States game?

75

What song did Phoebe sing at Mike's piano bar?

76

Where was Monica when she told her parents about her relationship with Richard?

77

What song was Rachel singing while walking around the apartment naked?

78

After Chandler's boss got divorced, what lie did Chandler tell him to avoid going to dinner with him and Monica?

79

What did Ross get caught doing in college that he blamed on Chandler?

80

How did Rachel's boss Joanna die?

81

What was Ben's first word?

75

"We Are the Champions"

76

At her father's birthday party

77

"Love to Love You Baby"

78

That he broke up with Monica

79

Smoking pot

80

She was hit by a cab

81

Hi

82

What is Joey's agent's full name?

83

What is the name of the hospital where Rachel gives birth to Emma?

84

At Monica's Sweet 16 party, who did Rachel go to third base with?

85

Who was the downstairs neighbor that died after complaining that Monica and
Rachel were stomping?

86

What actor played Sandy, the male nanny?

87

Who was responsible for getting Ross and Emily together?

88

What day did Chandler quit his job in Tulsa?

89
What was the name of the woman who was watching everyone with her
telescope?

90
Which two Friends got thrown out of a casino in Las Vegas?

91
What was the name of the restaurant where Chandler and Joey first meet
Phoebe's twin Ursula?

92
On Monica's seat chart display for her wedding, what color pins were Chandler's
guests?

93
What did Joey have at Ross's wedding that he promised Phoebe he wouldn't eat?

94
According to Chandler, what magic story do you use when you want to have sex?

95
What was the name of Monica's imaginary boyfriend from high school?

96

What was the name of Chandler's coworker that thought he was gay?

97

Where was everyone going away for the weekend when Phoebe's water broke?

98

What happened when the power saw got away from Joey?

99

In the opening credits, who turns off the lamp?

100

On what day did Ross and Rachel go on their break?

101

What caused the fire in Rachel and Phoebe's apartment?

102

What were Joey and Ross doing on the roof when they got locked up there?

103
What was the name of Mike's girlfriend that he broke up with to be with Phoebe?

104
What did Monica pay $25 for and have to wait in line at City Hall for three hours?

105
Who played Amanda, the woman who once lived in the building that Monica and
Phoebe were trying to avoid?

106
What was the first song the stripper danced to at Phoebe's party?

107
What was written on the t-shirt Ross wanted back from Rachel?

108
What did Phoebe hand out to guests at her grandmother's funeral?

109
What high school did Monica, Ross and Rachel go to?

110
On the Valentine's Day that Monica and Chandler decided to make their gifts, what did Monica give that Phoebe actually made and first offered to Chandler?

111
What part did Joey get and then was fired from in the Al Pacino movie?

112
What did Ross do to Rachel when they flew to Las Vegas together?

113
What did Joey use as luggage when everyone went to the beach in Montauk?

114
What kind of camp did Monica escape from?

115
What was the first thing Ross helped himself to from the hotel in Vermont?

116
Who played Joey's stalker Erica?

110
A sock bunny

111
His butt double

112
He drew a mustache on her

113
A paper bag

114
Fat camp

115
Apples

116
Brooke Shields

117

Who does Chandler run into just as he is about to give a sperm sample?

118

Which female soccer player does Rachel consider annoying?

119

What kind of car did Joey find keys for and then pretend it was his car?

120

What was the name of the guy Rachel was dating that was stealing from her?

121

What was Joey's character's name on the infomercial for the Milk Master 2000?

122

What U2 song did Ross have played on the radio to apologize to Rachel?

123

What soundtrack does Chandler have two copies of?

124

Joey got the lead in a TV show called Mac and C.H.E.E.S.E. What did C.H.E.E.S.E.
stand for?

125

Where was Ross traveling to that he couldn't go to Rachel's birthday barbeque?

126

Who gave Emma her name?

127

What is Joey's favorite food?

128

Who played Rachel's sister Amy?

129

Who did the animal control agent shoot with a tranquilizer dart?

130

In Monica's kitchen, she has a utensil holder that says homemade pickles and a
price. What is that price?

124
Computerized Humanoid Electronically Enhanced Secret Enforcer

125
China

126
Monica

127
Sandwiches

128
Christina Applegate

129
Phoebe

130
One cent

131

Phoebe told Rachel there are things about her that she should know. Number one, her friends are the most important thing in her life. Two, she never lies. What was the third thing?

132

What song was Ross learning to play on the bagpipes?

133

Who did Ross initially ask to be his best man at his wedding with Emily?

134

Who was the first episode of season eight dedicated to?

135

What did Monica accidentally book for Chandler after he found out that she had a bachelorette party?

136

What news did Fun Bobby share with everyone at the New Year's Eve Party?

137

What was the name of the food inspector that Phoebe dated?

131

She makes the best oatmeal raisin cookies in the world

132

"Celebration"

133

Chandler

134

The people of New York City

135

A hooker

136

His grandfather died

137

Larry

138
What did the group use to poke Ugly Naked Guy when they thought he was dead?

139
Who had the tip of his toe chopped off in the Gellar's kitchen on Thanksgiving?

140
What did Ross send Rachel at Bloomingdale's on her first week that caused them to fight?

141
Ross's first wife Carol was played by Jane Sibbett for the entire run of the show, except for one episode. Who played Carol on that single episode?

142
When Monica was six years old, she got her first bicycle. What happened when she sat on it?

143
Which musical act sang the theme song, "I'll Be There for You"?

144
When Charlie overheard Rachel and Phoebe talking in the fitting room, what did she get wrong?

145

When Ross tries to return his couch that he cut in half, how much does the
woman at the store offer him in store credit?

146

How did Phoebe propose to Mike?

147

What is the name of Joey's Cabbage Patch doll?

148

What was the name of the play that Joey did where he fell in love with Kate?

149

What did Rachel do at the end of the job interview at Ralph Lauren to the guy
interviewing her?

150

Who played eight-year-old Mackenzie, the girl who lived in the house Monica
and Chandler were buying?

151

Who made porn movies under the name Phoebe Buffay?

152

Where was the weirdest place that Phoebe had sex?

153

What was the name of the pizza delivery woman that Ross accused Chandler of flirting with?

154

Who couldn't tell time until she was 13-years-old?

155

Who handcuffed Chandler to her office chair?

156

Who was revealed to be Ross's mugger when he was a child?

157

How many women did Richard tell Monica he slept with?

158

What casino in Las Vegas did Joey work at, when the movie he was filming got shut down?

159

What did Phoebe buy Monica and Chandler as a wedding present?

160

Joey and Chandler's kitchen has a sign that reads Five Card Charlie Pays what?

161

Why does no one want to get Rachel as their Secret Santa?

162

Who had his hat stolen by a bully in Central Perk?

163

What "Three's Company" actress played Phoebe's grandmother?

164

Who took a cooking class with Monica after she received a bad review of her restaurant in the newspaper?

165

What did Joey buy at the silent auction that Rachel took him to?

159
A Ms. Pac-Man arcade game

160
5 to 1

161
She returns everything they buy her

162
Chandler

163
Audra Lindley

164
Joey

165
A sail boat

166

What part did Joey play in the porn movie he was in?

167

What was the name of the man Ross made up and told Mike that Phoebe
supposedly had a long-term relationship with?

168

Who was Joey making a movie with on the day he overslept and smelled?

169

What song did Chandler sing after inhaling helium after Rachel's birthday party?

170

When Joey asked Phoebe what stage name he should use, what did she suggest?

171

Who was about to get married in Las Vegas when they discovered that Ross and
Rachel just got married?

172

What did Ross step on when he walked into the Lamaze class?

173
Who played Monica and Ross's cousin Cassie that Ross tried to kiss?

174
What did Rachel forget when she went to the airport to fly to London for Ross
and Emily's wedding?

175
What did Chandler wear back from his honeymoon that Monica did not like?

176
What famous singer's son was in Ben's class?

177
Who did Ross hook up with when he found out that Emily was getting remarried?

178
Who is the replacement doctor that delivered Phoebe's babies a big fan of?

179
What kind of bed was incorrectly delivered to Monica?

173
Denise Richards

174
Her passport

175
A shell necklace

176
Sting

177
Janice

178
Fonzie from "Happy Days"

179
A race car bed

180
Who tried to teach Joey how to play guitar?

181
What food did Rachel order during her fight with Ross after she found out he
cheated on her?

182
What was the name of the student that Ross dated from the class he was
teaching?

183
What name did Joey give to his recliner?

184
Chandler tells Mike that Monica gets crazy competing. He says he has a scar on
his face from what game that they played?

185
Who had to kiss several times while playing spin the bottle at the bon voyage
party for Emily?

186
What did Ross make for the dinner with Charlie, Joey and Rachel that he burned
his hands on?

187
Who played Officer Good Body, the stripper at Phoebe's bachelorette party?

188
After Ross and Monica's Aunt Sylvia dies, what does Monica inherit from her?

189
Why did Ursula not want to go to her grandmother's funeral?

190
What was the name of the foreign exchange student from Thailand that went to school with Ross?

191
On the mix tape Chandler told Monica he made for her, who sings on it?

192
Who did Monica, Rachel and Phoebe watch from across the street after he accidentally got their pizza delivery?

193
Who bought Rachel's cat for $1,500?

187
Danny DeVito

188
A dollhouse

189
She had tickets to a concert

190
Ta-Taka-Ki-Kek

191
Janice

192
George Stephanopoulos

193
Gunther

194
When Monica was planning her wedding, she used her wedding book she had since was a child. What was the band that she wanted to play at her wedding in the sixth grade?

195
How many pages was the letter that Rachel wrote Ross at the beach house?

196
What was the name of Mike's friend that he asked to keep him away from Phoebe after their breakup?

197
Who played Dr. Richard Burke?

198
What was Emma's first word?

199
What does Monica do when she gets massages?

200
What did Rachel run into when she was running the way Phoebe does in the park?

201
What was the name of the woman Ross thought he was dating, but was actually babysitting for her?

202
Who pretends to be Joey's agent after he misses an audition?

203
What is Joey's middle name?

204
Who did Phoebe and Monica forget to invite to Rachel's baby shower?

205
Who did Rachel kiss on the night Monica and Chandler got engaged that made Monica mad?

206
Who did Phoebe confuse Demi Moore with when Monica asked her to cut her hair like the actress?

207
Where does Chandler agree to transfer to when he falls asleep in a company meeting?

201
Amanda

202
Phoebe

203
Francis

204
Rachel's mother

205
Ross

206
Dudley Moore

207
Tulsa, Oklahoma

208
Who did Monica fire at the restaurant to get the staff to respect her?

209
What did Wallace Pinscher, Monica and Rachel's friend from high school, do for Rachel?

210
What rockstar played Stephanie, the professional musician who got Phoebe bumped from Central Perk?

211
When Chandler was moving in with Monica, Joey took out an ad for a new roommate. What did it say?

212
What was the name of the woman that Joey's father was having an affair with?

213
Who watched Ben while Ross had a meeting and taught him a bunch of pranks?

214
Who played the vendor who sold Joey the hat with the British flag on it in London?

208
Joey

209
He took the SATs for her

210
Chrissie Hynde

211
Wanted female roommate, non-smoker, non-ugly

212
Ronny

213
Rachel

214
Richard Branson

215

What does Joey's costar in his war movie, played by Gary Oldman, keep doing
that annoys him?

216

What event led producers to reshoot several scenes in the airport where Chandler
makes inappropriate jokes?

217

What happened to the guy that Monica "Woo Hoo"ed on the street?

218

What happened to Phoebe when she was telling the group about her
Thanksgiving in a past life?

219

What happened when Ross was showing Chandler how to play racquetball on the
stairs?

220

What game did Joey and Chandler make up while Joey was trying to write a
script?

221

What did Monica's coworker Julio write a poem about while they were fooling
around?

215
Keeps spitting on him

216
The September 11th, 2001 attacks

217
He got hit by an ambulance

218
Her arm was blown off

219
He hit a girl and broke her leg

220
Fire Ball

221
An empty vase

222
What did Monica make for all the neighbors and leave in a basket on the apartment door?

223
When Phoebe didn't want Rachel to know she worked at a corporate massage parlor and was forced to give her a massage, she pretended to be Swedish. What name did she use?

224
What did Emily convince Ross to get that Joey and Chandler made fun of?

225
What was the name of the artwork that Mike wanted Phoebe to get rid of?

226
Who played Erica, the pregnant woman that Monica and Chandler were adopting her baby?

227
What was the name of the discount wedding dress store where Monica fought a woman for her dress?

228
While Monica and Phoebe were planning Rachel's surprise party, what did Monica put Phoebe in charge of?

229
What company did Rachel interview for in the same restaurant that her boss at Ralph Lauren was eating in?

230
Why did Rachel's father cut off her sister Jill?

231
Who did Rachel meet in the building during the blackout?

232
What show did Joey's grandmother come over to watch him on that he wound up being cut out of?

233
Who entered a Vanilla Ice lookalike contest and won?

234
What is the name of the pizzeria that is written on most of the pizza boxes throughout the series?

235
Why was the crowd cheering so much for Monica when she sang at the piano bar?

229
Gucci

230
Because she bought a boat, for a friend

231
Paolo

232
"Law and Order"

233
Chandler

234
Ray Bari Pizza

235
They could see through her shirt when the spotlight came on

236
What song did Phoebe shoot a music video for?

237
What did Monica give Chandler for their one-year dating anniversary?

238
What did Ross wear to help him get between classes he was teaching?

239
When Rachel made dessert on Thanksgiving the pages on the recipe stuck together and she had half an English Trifle. What was the other half?

240
What newspaper did Monica get a job writing restaurant reviews for?

241
What did Phoebe hit with the cab when she went to see her father the second time?

242
What was the name of the Ross lookalike that Rachel briefly dated?

243
While waiting for Rachel to give birth, Chandler and Monica decide to try and have a baby. What does Chandler call it when Monica starts counting on her fingers?

244
What did Elizabeth do to Ross after he broke up with her?

245
What did Monica take from her restaurant that got her fired?

246
When Monica surprises Chandler in Tulsa, what does she mistakenly think he was molesting himself to?

247
What did Emily's friends invite Ross to play with them?

248
Who played Gavin, the man who replaced Rachel when she was on maternity leave?

249
What zoo does Marcel wind up going to?

243
Period math

244
She hit him with a water balloon

245
Five steaks

246
Shark porn

247
Rugby

248
Dermot Mulroney

249
San Diego Zoo

250
In the first episode of season six, each cast member had the same last name
added to their name to celebrate Courtney Cox's marriage. What was that last name?

251
Who taught Monica, Rachel and Phoebe how to play poker?

252
Who got a ticket for driving too slow and then tried to flirt with the cop?

253
Who played Emily's stepmother Andrea Waltham?

254
What does Robert, Phoebe's boyfriend, do that everyone keeps noticing?

255
What was Phoebe's New Year's resolution for 1999

256
Who scored the first touchdown when everyone played football on Thanksgiving?

250
Arquette

251
Aunt Iris

252
Ross

253
Jennifer Saunders

254
Falling out of his shorts

255
To pilot a commercial jet

256
Joey

257

What does Monica lose in the hotel room when she went away with Chandler, that helps Joey figure out that they were dating?

258

What is Rachel's middle name?

259

What did Gunther dress up as for Chandler and Monica's Halloween party?

260

What was the color of the sweater that Phoebe said belonged to the father of Rachel's baby?

261

Who played Paul Stevens, the father of Ross's girlfriend?

262

Who showed up to their 30th birthday party drunk?

263

What hairstyle did Monica get in Barbados?

257
An eye lash curler

258
Karen

259
Charlie Brown

260
Red

261
Bruce Willis

262
Monica

263
Corn rows

264
What craving did Phoebe get while pregnant?

265
Why won't Chandler have sex with Monica in the bathroom?

266
What three posters of musical acts did Rachel have on her childhood bedroom walls?

267
What did Chandler get when he tried to return the chick?

268
What does Rachel call Ross after he tries to befriend Ugly Naked Guy to get his apartment?

269
What did Phoebe and Ross discover when they got to the airport after chasing Rachel before she left for Paris?

270
Who wound up dancing on MTV during Spring Break?

264
Meat

265
Because that's where people make number two

266
Shaun Cassidy, Duran Duran and The Thompson Twins

267
A duck

268
Naked Ross

269
They were at JFK Airport and Rachel was at Newark Airport

270
Ross

271

What is the intersection of the apartment building where Monica, Rachel, Chandler and Joey live?

272

Why did Phoebe break up with Gary?

273

What was the name of Rachel's assistant that she took a Polaroid of at his interview?

274

Who peed on Monica when she got stung by a jelly fish?

275

Where did Joey and Monica drive to in order to buy lottery tickets?

276

What musician played the man who hired Phoebe to play songs for kids at the library?

277

Where did Joey have his "Days of Our Lives" party?

278
Where did Ross leave his pink shirt, or as he called it, faded salmon?

279
What did Chandler swallow after Monica and Phoebe told him not to give the triplets a Kron action figure because they might swallow small parts?

280
Which of the women did Gunther kiss?

281
What actor played Malcolm, Ursula's stalker who started dating Phoebe?

282
Who catered Carol and Susan's wedding?

283
When Joey is asked to do an interview with Soap Opera digest, Rachel wants him to mention her by what name?

284
Who came into the restaurant where Chandler was just about to propose to Monica?

278
Mona's apartment

279
A sonic blaster gun

280
Phoebe

281
David Arquette

282
Monica

283
Gal Pal Rachel Green

284
Richard

285

Who did Ross get off the plane from China with?

286

Who catches Monica and Chandler having sex in the hospital after Rachel gives birth?

287

Which Friend once lived in Prague?

288

What was the name of Chandler's assistant in Tulsa who had a lot of cats?

289

Who was watching Marcel when he got out?

290

What was the thing Phoebe was singing about, that she found in her bed?

291

What actress played Joey's mother?

285
Julie

286
Monica's father

287
Phoebe

288
Jo Lynn

289
Rachel

290
A little black curly hair

291
Brenda Vaccaro

292

The night Monica and Chandler had sex in London, who was she actually looking for to have sex with?

293

What was Rachel wearing when Joshua came to the door after she freaked him out by talking about getting married?

294

What did Rachel give Chandler to help him quit smoking?

295

When Joey got Phoebe work on his show as an extra, what was the first role she played?

296

In a flashback episode what was Ugly Naked Guy called?

297

What one condition did Emily have if she came back to New York to work on her marriage with Ross?

298

What did Joey become a model for all over New York City?

299
Who played Will, Monica's fat friend from high school who lost 150 pounds?

300
Why does Ross like to go to the Hard Rock Café?

301
What was the name of Ross and Monica's cousin who didn't invite Monica to her wedding?

302
When Joey was dating Charlie, she wanted to explore the city and asked to go somewhere that Joey confused with a New York sports team. Where did Charlie want to go?

303
What did Monica and Rachel have to do to get their apartment back?

304
Where did Phoebe and Rachel take Emma on Thanksgiving dressed up like a cow girl?

305
What did Sara, Phoebe's friend that Joey dated, do that annoyed him?

299
Brad Pitt

300
He likes the "Purple Rain" display

301
Frannie

302
The Metropolitan Museum of Art

303
They had to kiss for one minute

304
To a beauty pageant

305
She ate French Fries from his plate

306

When Pete was away on business, he told Monica that they had to talk. What did he tell her when he got home?

307

Who plays Katie, the woman Joey dated, that Rachel kicked?

308

What kind of ghosts is Joey afraid of?

309

After Joey's cable and phone are cut off, where does he take a job?

310

What was the name of Joey's girlfriend that Chandler was in love with?

311

Who accidentally erased a message from Emily on Ross's machine the night before she was getting remarried?

312

Why did Chandler break up with his childhood friend Julie when they went to camp together?

306
That he wanted to become the Ultimate Fighting Champion

307
Soleil Moon Frye

308
Little girl ghosts

309
At Central Perk

310
Kathy

311
Rachel

312
Because she got fat

313
What did the robber write on the Etch a Sketch after stealing everything in Joey and Chandler's apartment, while Joey was locked in the entertainment unit?

314
What did Phoebe think her kids with Mike would be named?

315
After going to a Knicks game with Richard what did Chandler start growing?

316
Who played Joey's identical hand twin?

317
What did Monica give Chandler to butch up his bath?

318
What TV Show did Janine invite Ross and Monica to dance on?

319
What was the first name of Gandalf, the man Chandler and Ross wanted to party with?

320
What did Monica make in place of birthday cake for Rachel's party?

321
Where did Ross and Rachel have their first kiss after they had a fight about both
not telling each other that they like one another?

322
What was the name of the character that Debi Mazar played in the episode where
Rachel is about to give birth?

323
What is Ross allergic to that made his tongue swell after he ate Monica's pie?

324
Who ate ding dongs without taking the tin foil off?

325
After Bloomingdale's eliminated Rachel's department, what did she become at
the store?

326
What is the name of the rat that lives in Phoebe cupboard that freaked Mike out?

327
What name does Monica use when she meets the woman who stole her credit card?

328
Who drove home with Joey from Las Vegas?

329
What did Phoebe give Ursula for their birthday?

330
When Joey got a call back for a movie and was asked to do nudity, what did he lie about?

331
Who did Joey meet in London while trying to find Buckingham Palace?

332
Who did Monica run into at the video store when she had panties stuck to her leg?

333
What book did Phoebe and Rachel have to read for their class they were taking at the New School that Rachel thought she read in high school but didn't?

327
Manana

328
Phoebe

329
A Judy Jetson thermos

330
He told the casting director that he was uncircumcised

331
Sarah, The Duchess of York. AKA Fergie

332
Richard

333
"Wuthering Heights"

334
Who insulted Monica by saying cheater, cheater, compulsive eater?

335
Who was slapped by George Michael when he rushed the stage at a Wham concert?

336
What TV theme song did everyone start humming on the couch in Central Perk?

337
Where did Joey get the crib, he brought into the apartment to show Rachel, he wanted her to stay?

338
What lost things were Chandler and Ross looking for the day after Chandler and Monica's wedding?

339
Who played Earl, the guy Phoebe called from her telemarketing job, who wanted to kill himself?

340
What did Charlie return to Joey that he left at her apartment that Ross thought Joey was giving him?

334
Ross

335
Chandler

336
"The Odd Couple"

337
He found it on the street

338
Disposable cameras

339
Jason Alexander

340
A toothbrush, underwear and a Van Halen CD

341
What was written on the Etch a Sketch when Joey and Chandler had free porn?

342
What did Rachel do after her first date with Joey when he ran his hand up her
leg?

343
What language did Phoebe try and teach Joey for his audition but he just couldn't
get it?

344
In Monica's kitchen what does the time read on the "Cookie Time" cookie jar?

345
What did Ross send to Ugly Naked Guy to try and get him to sublet him his
apartment?

346
Who told Rachel he loved her in Central Perk before she left for Paris?

347
When Joey's refrigerator broke, how much was he trying to get everyone to pay
for their half?

341
Knock knock...who's there? PORN!

342
She slapped him

343
French

344
4 O'clock

345
A basket of mini muffins

346
Gunther

347
$400

348

On what ride at the Magic Kingdom did Ross and Carol have sex?

349

What kind of pet did Rachel pay a thousand dollars for and then regret it?

350

Who did Chandler accidentally give a lap dance to in the steam room?

351

What was the name of the woman Ross was dating that Rachel convinced to shave her head again?

352

What position did Chandler get after he was passed over for one of the three assistant jobs at the ad agency?

353

What did Ross do to Rachel on their first date that made her laugh?

354

Who played the role of Charlie Wheeler?

348
It's a Small World After All

349
A pure-bred show quality Sphynx cat

350
Monica's father

351
Bonnie

352
Junior copywriter

353
He touched her butt

354
Aisha Tyler

355
What does the label say on the video tape that Chandler mistakes for porn but is actually Phoebe's friend giving birth?

356
What did Joey call Janine's curling iron?

357
Who played the sloppy girl Cheryl that Ross dated?

358
What song did Monica and Chandler dance to after they got engaged?

359
What fantasy did Ross reveal to Rachel after they talked of him wearing the Navy outfit for her?

360
What was the name of the game show Joey had an audition for to be the host?

361
What did Joey and Phoebe taste that grossed out Ross?

355
Candy and Cookie

356
The really hot stick

357
Rebecca Romijn

358
"Wonderful Tonight"

359
Princess Leia in a gold bikini from "Return of the Jedi"

360
Bamboozle

361
Breast milk

362
What is Ross's birthday?

363
According to Monica while giving Chandler advice on sex, how many basic
erogenous zones does a woman have?

364
When Phoebe met Mike's parents, she told them she once had hepatitis. How did
she get it?

365
Two actresses played the role of Mindy. One was Jana Marie Hupp. Who was the
other actress?

366
What one item in Monica's kitchen belongs to Rachel?

367
What did Ross say when his date asked him to talk dirty?

368
What was the name of the band Chandler wanted for his wedding?

369
Where was Ross and Emily supposed to honeymoon, that Rachel wound up going to alone?

370
How did Frank Jr. meet Alice?

371
At the New Year's Eve party heading into 1999, Monica and Chandler kissed at midnight. Who did Ross and Joey kiss?

372
What did Phoebe think would happen if she went to the dentist?

373
Who played Chandler's mother?

374
What rumor about Rachel was known all over her school and even in Chandler's high school?

375
What does Ross dress up as after he couldn't get a Santa outfit?

369
Greece

370
She was his home economics teacher

371
Joey kissed Rachel and Ross kissed Phoebe

372
Someone would die

373
Morgan Fairchild

374
That she was the hermaphrodite cheerleader from Long Island

375
The holiday armadillo

376
What is Chandler's middle name?

377
What did the email say that Chandler opened on Ross's computer that had a virus
and erased his hard drive?

378
Who did Emily show around London that made Ross uncomfortable?

379
What did Joey make Chandler do to make up for lying about watching his demo
tape?

380
In what area did Monica and Chandler buy a house?

381
Where did Ross go on his spring break in college?

382
Who does Chandler get stuck in a bank vestibule with during the blackout?

376
Muriel

377
Nude pictures of Anna Kournikova

378
Susan

379
He made him wear the Japanese lipstick for men

380
Westchester

381
To Egypt with his Dad

382
Jill Goodacre

383
What was Joey really trying to save when he covered Ross when he thought he heard a gunshot?

384
Who did Monica put in the picture with her to announce her engagement after Chandler made weird faces when trying to smile?

385
What does Joey have to do with the super after he almost gets Monica and Rachel evicted?

386
What did Joey tell Chandler he loaned Monica $2,000 for?

387
What book did all the women read that caused them to blame men for their problems?

388
Where did Phoebe work in her first job?

389
What was Rachel's first choice for a baby name if it was a girl?

383
His sandwich

384
Joey

385
Be his dancing partner

386
A boob job

387
"Be Your Own Wind Keeper"

388
Dairy Queen

389
Sandrine

390

What was the name of the chocolate substitute that Monica was asked to make recipes for when she had a job interview?

391

What magazine did Ross send a joke into that was printed, but Chandler said it was his joke?

392

What is Joey's personal best for the number of Oreos he stuffed in his mouth?

393

What song did Rachel sing at Barry and Mindy's wedding?

394

What does Rachel's doctor suggest she do after she is overdue having the baby?

395

What concert did Monica, Chandler and Ross go to for Ross's birthday?

396

What was the name of the guy from Monica's new job that she said was the funniest guy she ever met?

390
Mockolate

391
Playboy

392
Fifteen

393
"Copacabana"

394
Have sex

395
Hootie and the Blowfish

396
Jeffrey

397

What was the name of the dance that Monica and Ross did in middle school and got honorable mention in the brother-sister dance category?

398

After Chandler's breakup with Kathy, who took him to a strip club to cheer him up?

399

What name did Joey use when he went to get his eyebrows waxed?

400

When Ross started doing a guest lecturer series at NYU, what did he do to make it interesting?

401

Where does Monica meet the woman who stole her credit card?

402

What song did Marcel keep playing on the poker episode?

403

Who played Melissa, the woman Rachel kissed in college?

404
What happened to Phoebe's regular doctor that she could not get to the hospital
to deliver the triplets?

405
How old was Ethan, the younger guy Monica was dating?

406
What was the name of Phoebe's former singing partner who showed up at
Central Perk?

407
What sport did Chandler and Monica play with his boss and his wife that
Chandler intentionally lost and made Monica mad?

408
Who did Rachel serve her last cup of coffee to as a waitress at the coffee house?

409
What was the name of Chandler's previous roommate that left after they bought
a hibachi together?

410
Who played Ursula's fiancé Eric?

404
She fell in the shower and hit her head

405
Seventeen

406
Leslie

407
Tennis

408
Chandler

409
Kip

410
Sean Penn

411
What did Monica get from her father after he ruined all the boxes that contained
her childhood items?

412
Who played Rachel's date that she took to Joey's opening night after she found
out Ross was bringing a date?

413
When Phoebe pretends to seduce Chandler, Joey tells her show to what article of
clothing that he is afraid of?

414
Where in the world was Rachel offered a job working for Louis Vuitton?

415
Who walked Ross down the aisle at Monica and Chandler's wedding?

416
Who wound up beating Mike in Ping Pong?

417
What does Emily say to Ross after he says he loves her at the airport?

411
His Porsche

412
Ben Stiller

413
Her bra

414
Paris

415
Rachel and Phoebe

416
Chandler

417
Thank you

418
What did Monica and Chandler give each other for their first wedding
anniversary?

419
Who was Monica's midnight mystery kisser when she visited Ross and Chandler
at college?

420
In the what could have been episode, what did Ross do during his threesome with
Carol and Susan?

421
What did Monica's parents spend the "Monica Wedding Fund" on?

422
Where did Ross end up on the train when he fell asleep, while dating the woman
in Poughkeepsie?

423
What animal does Phoebe believe has the spirit of her mother Lily?

424
Who played Susie Moss from Chandler's fourth grade class that he ran into on a
movie set?

418
Monica gave Chandler a $500 watch and he wrote her a rap song

419
Ross

420
Ate a sandwich

421
A beach house

422
Montreal

423
A cat

424
Julia Roberts

425
Who accidentally dropped the lottery tickets off the balcony?

426
What did Ross leave himself a message on his answering machine to remind himself to buy that Monica and Rachel overheard?

427
What food does Chandler like, especially on a barbeque chicken pizza that Monica does not?

428
What does Monica have to wear on Thanksgiving after getting ice in her eye?

429
Who played Ryan, Phoebe's old Navy boyfriend?

430
In the interview with Soap Opera Digest, Joey confuses the word mentor with what candy?

431
What does Rachel discover when she takes Emma to a new doctor?

425
Phoebe

426
Stamps

427
Sun dried tomatoes

428
An eye patch

429
Charlie Sheen

430
Mentos

431
That Ross still sees his childhood pediatrician

432
After the owner of the dry cleaner refused to put Joey's picture on the wall, he took the woman in the store out for dinner. Who was she?

433
What was the name of Joey's tailor who touched Chandler?

434
What was the first thing Rachel said she won't miss about living with Monica?

435
Where did Chandler tell Janice he was moving to because his job was relocating?

436
What did Phoebe eat at Mike's parents' house that made her sick?

437
Who showed up at Benihana on Valentine's Day while Ross was on a date?

438
What award was Joey nominated for his role on "Days of Our Lives"?

439
What was the name of the place where Ross and Emily got married?

440
What did Monica think the maid Chandler hired stole from her?

441
Whose mother did Ross kiss?

442
What did Chandler do when he saw Janice and her husband skating at Rockefeller Center?

443
At Christmas, Phoebe was collecting money for charity with a bell and bucket in front of what store?

444
Why did Ginger break up with Chandler?

445
When Joey is trying to come up with a stage name, what does Chandler suggest?

439
Montgomery Hall

440
Her jeans and bra

441
Chandler's

442
Whipped a kid's pretzel at them

443
Macy's

444
Because she was grossed out by his third nipple

445
Joseph Stalin

446

What does Phoebe say after Rachel tells her they should starts a new friend group, since they are the best ones?

447

Who taught Phoebe how to ride a bike?

448

Who does Rachel fix her boss Joanna up with?

449

What did Phoebe find under the cushions at Central Perk when she was looking for change for a tip?

450

When Chandler had to break the news to Monica that they might not be able to have kids, how did he describe her uterus?

451

What is Phoebe's most common alias?

452

What phobia did Joshua reveal the night he and Rachel had a romantic dinner?

453

What happened to Rachel at the playground when she was four years old?

454

What is Joey's policy on sharing food?

455

What movie made Monica, Joey and Phoebe cry, but not Chandler?

456

Who did Chandler kiss in a dark Atlantic City bar?

457

What was the first play that Rachel saw Joey in?

458

What is the name of the woman at the gym that they bring out when Chandler tries to cancel his membership and also gets Ross to sign up?

459

What was the name of Chandler's new roommate after Joey moved out?

453

She had a traumatic swing incident when her hair got stuck in the chain and had
to be cut out

454

JOEY DOESN'T SHARE FOOD!

455

"E.T."

456

A very pretty guy

457

"Freud!"

458

Maria

459

Eddie

460

In the dream Monica told Rachel about, what did she do to Mayor McCheese on their wedding night?

461

Where did Ross and Rachel tell everybody that they were having a girl?

462

What did Chandler do to make up to Joey for kissing Kathy?

463

What did Joey and Chandler drink from Monica's refrigerator that they both thought was cider?

464

What does Rachel tell Joey is her big work problem, when she tries to get him talking after they feel awkward around each other?

465

Who was responsible for fixing up Phoebe with Mike, by saying that they were old friends?

466

What did Phoebe's husband Duncan do for a living?

460
She ate his head

461
In the bathroom

462
Locked himself in a box

463
Fat

464
That her boss wants to buy her baby

465
Joey

466
Professional Ice Dancer

467

What did Ross do to himself to prepare for his date with Hillary, Monica's coworker?

468

Who played Chandler's father?

469

What is the only way Monica eats tic tacs?

470

What was the name of the woman at Chandler's job in Tulsa, that was the runner up Miss Oklahoma and came on to him?

471

What did Joey use as his Thanksgiving pants after he promised Monica he would eat an entire turkey?

472

Where did David, Phoebe's boyfriend, moved to?

473

What was the name of the 1950's theme diner that Monica worked at?

467
Whitened his teeth

468
Kathleen Turner

469
In even numbers

470
Wendy

471
Phoebe's maternity pants

472
Minsk

473
Moondance

474
Chandler met Marjorie when he took Joey to the sleep clinic. Why was she there?

475
Where did Rachel invite everyone except Ross to go after their breakup?

476
Who played the role of the man who dropped a condom in Phoebe's guitar case when she was singing outside Central Perk and also returned as her brother in future episodes?

477
What did Joey name the new chick and duck he got for Monica and Chandler as a housewarming gift?

478
What was the last think Phoebe accomplished before she turned 30, before finding out she was 31?

479
What does Katie, the woman Joey is dating, keep doing that annoys him?

480
Where did Ross tell Joey that he and Charlie kissed?

474
She talks in her sleep

475
To her sister's cabin to go skiing

476
Giovanni Ribisi

477
Chick Jr. and Duck Jr.

478
She did one mile on a Hippity Hop

479
Punching him

480
On the plane heading home from Barbados

481
Who did Phoebe says was the father of her baby when she lied to protect Rachel's secret that she was pregnant?

482
What did the writers on "Days of Our Lives" do when Joey said he wrote some of his own lines?

483
What happened to Ross at Nana's funeral?

484
Who snuggled and napped together on the couch after watching "Die Hard"?

485
When Joey was auditioning for a movie Warren Beatty was directing, what did he have to do?

486
What did Chandler do when Joey took him to the premiere of his movie "Over There"?

487
Who brought a security blanket to college and used the excuse that it was a wall hanging?

481
James Brolin

482
They killed his character off the show

483
He fell in an open grave

484
Ross and Joey

485
Kiss another man

486
He falls asleep during the movie

487
Chandler

488
After Chandler broke up with a girl who had big nostrils, Joey told of a girl he broke up with because she had what?

489
What was the name of Chandler's employee that he was supposed to fire but couldn't do it?

490
Who did Phoebe make out with at Rachel's job who lied and said he was Ralph Lauren?

491
Who played Kristen Lang, the woman both Joey and Ross were dating that just moved onto the block?

492
What song makes Emma laugh?

493
What candy do both Ross and Emily bring home that Joey eats?

494
What was the name of the woman Ross slept with when he and Rachel were on a break?

488
A huge Adam's apple

489
Nina

490
Kenny, the copy guy

491
Gabrielle Union

492
"Baby Got Back"

493
Toblerone

494
Chloe

495
What was the name of the guy Monica ran into from high school that asked her
out and Rachel thought he left her a message?

496
Why doesn't Ross like ice cream?

497
When Ross moves into his new apartment, a neighbor shows up to ask him to
give $100 for Howard's retirement. What does Howard do in the building?

498
What was the name of the club that Ross was part of in high school with Will,
who had issues with Rachel?

499
What brand of refrigerator did Monica have in her apartment?

500
Which character speaks the last line of the series

495
Chip Matthews

496
It's too cold

497
He is the handyman

498
The I hate Rachel Green club

499
International Harvester

500
Chandler